Suicide Con

Stanley Mullen

Alpha Editions

This edition published in 2024

ISBN : 9789364737760

Design and Setting By
Alpha Editions
www.alphaedis.com
Email - info@alphaedis.com

As per information held with us this book is in Public Domain.
This book is a reproduction of an important historical work. Alpha Editions uses the best technology to reproduce historical work in the same manner it was first published to preserve its original nature. Any marks or number seen are left intentionally to preserve its true form.

SUICIDE COMMAND

By STANLEY MULLEN

The rookie astrogator's fingers itched for the controls of a ship. But he never asked for the privilege of riding an atomic bomb into the heart of hell!

Messages crackled through the black gulf of space—the Interplanetary Distress Call. Blaze Norman, navigation officer of the ISP cruiser Scorpio, came out of his space-fog and stared at the helioflash board which was suddenly ablaze with light. Harald, the operator, grunted and spun dials as the frantic messages clicked off.

"What's up, Harald?" Norman asked.

Harald waved him away impatiently and crouched over his helio receiver board. He was a grizzled old spacehound and hated working with rookie officers. Good kids all right—the examinations saw to that—but you never knew how they were going to react, how much you could depend on them in an emergency. And this was an emergency—

Out in the bleak void between the orbits of Jupiter and Saturn, the spaceliner Tellus was breaking up. Half of her starboard batteries had fused and exploded, that was just the beginning. Before needle-valves could be shut off, streams of free neutrons ran up the fuel lines into the secondary bank of preparation tanks. Radiation counters buzzed angrily as primary degeneration spread through the masses of fuel in the leaden containers. The lead walls buckled and gave way. Tons of molten magma deluged all of the after compartments of the titanic luxury liner. Inferno.

Tellus jerked like a nervous racehorse as the rest of her stern rocket tubes froze and exploded. The after third of the ship was blasted out of existence. Heaven knew what would happen when the rest of that degenerating metal reached the stage of instantaneous disintegration.

"It's the spaceliner Tellus," Harald snapped. "She's in trouble outside Jupiter. Position 9-84-7. Two degrees N. Ecliptic. Range 11/4.7. Get on your charts and find out what's out there. I'll buzz the old man."

Captain Fries' face appeared on the televisor screen. "Never mind the details," he snapped. "We got part of it up here. Too faint for the audios, of course. What ships are in that sector?"

Lieutenant Blaze Norman glanced up from the chart panel. "Nothing of any kind closer than Ganymede, sir. And only some slow ore-freighters there. If there's anything else, my records don't show it."

Captain Fries' face looked suddenly old and tired. He sighed. "I guess we'll have to go, but I don't know what good a ship this size will do if they have to be taken off. Anything more from the Tellus?"

"Not much, sir," Harald told him curtly. "They seemed to be breaking up fast. Half the crew are already dead. No telling about the passengers. Operator thinks they may last five or six hours, but no more. If degeneration spreads through the whole ship, it won't be as long as that."

"I know. I know. What about lifeboats?"

"Nine of their ten are gone. The other won't hold a third of the survivors."

"Tell them to hold on. We're coming. Hang onto your hats, and don't forget the acceleration cushions."

Harald set his helioflash transmitter on the automatic relays and sent the message repeating endlessly across the darkness. He shot a calculating glance at Norman and wondered if he'd hold up in the mess that lay ahead. You never knew about these new men.

Scorpio had been inbound for Callisto. Alarms shrilled all through her slim torpedo shape. Acceleration warning. The two men in her communications room buckled on their shock cushions and braced themselves. The obsolescent cruiser groaned and began to labor as the standby batteries of rockets let go at full power. A drumming vibration beat through the ship. Indicator needles jerked past painted numerals. Barely perceptible at first, the steadily rising curve of acceleration built into nauseating paralysis.

Norman's face was pale and drawn. Harald grinned apishly, enjoying his companion's discomfiture. "Think she'll hold together at twenty Martian gravities?" he asked.

Norman realized he was being razzed, and by a subordinate, but he could only smile feebly. "This is one way to find out," he gasped. "How long d'you think it'll take us to get there?"

Harald shrugged. "Six hours. Maybe seven. Why'd you join up if you can't stand acceleration?"

"I didn't. They transferred me into it. They say you get used to it."

"Some never do. The old man's a killer that way."

Norman set his teeth grimly. "I'll get used to it."

Exactly five hours and twenty minutes later (Earth Time) a fleck of mirrored sunlight in the star-sprinkled darkness ahead gave evidence that the Tellus was still holding out. The Scorpio hammered up in a long, staggering glide, forward rockets bathing her nose with lurid glare at full negative acceleration. Weak and haggard from their incredible run, the ISP crew crawled to stations as the emergency alarms screamed.

The Tellus was in a bad way. The shattered hull was still spinning dangerously like an unbalanced top. Fiery drops of molten, disintegrating armor plate whirled into space in deadly showers. Crewmen of the spaceliner waged a losing battle to damp-out the holocaust raging in her stern compartments, and knots of men in clumsy space-suits clustered about the collapsing hull, deluging the plates with Rayburn's Isotope. But the cold of space was too great, and most of the liquified stabilizer dispersed in frost-flakes before it could act on the degenerating metal. Radiation from the masses of spitting magma astern went through the after half of the crippled liner like storms of deadly invisible bullets, striking down the men at their work through weak joints in their armor.

The Tellus was doomed.

It was ticklish work maneuvering close to the immense hulk, but Captain Fries ran the Scorpio alongside and made fast with magnetic grapnels. ISP men in grotesquely robot-like space-armor ran out the jointed airlock tube and attached it to the main hatch of the liner. Valves opened automatically as the pressure equalized.

Captain Fries and Lieutenant Norman were the first to board the doomed liner. They were met by a blood-spattered second officer.

"I'm Lore," he said. "The ranking officers are all dead. I'm in command."

"How many people have you?" Fries asked savagely.

Lore smiled grimly. "I was afraid you'd ask that. Too many for you, I'm afraid."

"We'll do all we can," Fries promised. "We've jettisoned everything we could spare. There's ammunition spread from here to .54, not to mention bedding, supplies, tools, spare parts and all but the bare minimum of fuel. At a squeeze, we can get about a hundred and forty people on the Scorpio besides our complement of twenty-eight men. I don't know what we'll do about the others."

Lore shook his head. "I can't tell you exactly how many are left. There's no use taking the ones who are too seriously burned. We have one lifeboat left. By jamming, we can get about eighty in it. You can tow it to Callisto."

"Any other officers left?"

"Merrill, our third ... if he's still alive. The last I saw, he was outside with the others, trying to damp-out the stuff. No use, of course. I guess you'd better take over. I've got mine."

Lore staggered and fell back against a bulkhead. Norman caught him and lowered him gently to the floor. Lore fought his blistered lids open, murmured, "Radiation burns," with lips that were strangely thickened. He jerked spasmodically, then a glaze of agony masked his eyes as he shuddered and lay still.

The main salon of the spaceliner was a charnel house. Dead and dying lay in rows, many of them in horribly grotesque attitudes reflecting the agony of their passing. A harried doctor was doing what could be done to relieve the unrelievable suffering. A group of passengers were huddled into a corner. Most of them were pale and dull-eyed, a few sobbed hysterically, some prayed. Norman began sorting them out.

"Women and children first. Married men next. We'll go over the injured while the rest of you get aboard the Scorpio. Any that have a chance to recover, we'll take. No crowding."

Fries shouted orders, then stood back out of the way while a stream of beaten and hopeless humanity filed through the airlock toward the Scorpio. One woman clung to her husband, screaming, until Norman took her gently by the arm and led her away. She moved like a sleep-walker and, though her lips twitched as if in speech, no sound came.

"Check everyone for radiation," Fries ordered gruffly. "We can't be too careful."

Merrill, the third officer, came in and started shedding his space-armor. He was lean, hard-looking, with a twisted, humorous face. "Anything I can do?" he asked curtly.

Fries stared at him blankly. "Get your burns taken care of, then get some of these people into the lifeboat if you're able."

Merrill shrugged and laughed. "Why bother to patch me up? There won't be room enough for all of us. I'll take care of it now; the lifeboat's ready."

Harald felt like a recording angel as he stood in the airlock counting off the people coming through. It was hideous.

"One-forty," he told Fries.

Most of the injured had gone into the lifeboat, but some of the men-passengers still remained in the saloon. Norman stared about him, estimating. One of the men was the husband of the woman who had refused to leave without him.

"Full up?" the man asked. Norman nodded. The passenger tried to smile, but his lips trembled.

Captain Fries stood by the airlock. Norman strode up to him, lips set in a thin line.

"I'd like permission to stay here and let someone have my place," he burst out. "There are other single men in your crew."

Captain Fries had aged years in that half hour. Soberly, he nodded. "Permission granted. But I haven't the right to ask the others. In fact, I haven't the right to grant your request but, unofficially, I'm proud of you."

"I'll ask them."

Harald ambled out of the airlock and made a weary gesture. "You won't have to. I've already done it. The men are ready as soon as you give orders for the rest of the passengers to come aboard."

Captain Fries gave the necessary commands, then turned to his own crew as they filed out of the airlock. His eyes glittered fiercely, as if a core of ice splintered the light within them. He tried to speak, but there was nothing more to do or say.

Merrill came back from supervising the loading of the lifeboat. "Oh, we've got company," he said roughly. "We'll be a cozy little group. I hope some of you can play cards. Any hope of other ships getting here?"

Fries shook his head. "Not in time. Some ore-freighters have left Ganymede, but it'll be two days before they can get here. I'm sorry, but I've done all I can...."

"I know. I'm glad you got all the passengers aboard. It's not so bad for the rest of us. That old black devil out there gets all of us spacerats sooner or later. Thanks for coming...."

Fries turned to his men and tried to speak. Harald shut him off roughly. "Sure, skipper, it's been nice knowing you. But no heroics. Hell ought to be cool after what this ship will be like when that stuff reaches critical mass. Now get the hell out of here before we blow...."

From the control room of the Tellus, Norman, Harald and Merrill watched the pinkish dot which was the Scorpio's rocket exhaust dwindle into the jet immensity of sky. Off there—somewhere—was the point where Jupiter's orbit would intersect the long curve of the cruiser's course. Jupiter. Ganymede. Safety.

"Well, I've always wanted to tell the skipper to go to—" Harald said lamely. "Now I feel somehow let down. How long do we have?"

"That depends. I'm no radiation engineer, but Failles says there are three possible routes of breakdown. If the ship holds together until then, we can expect to be blown to whatever you like in from six to ten hours. I'd say the ship will fall apart first, probably in less than three hours. Are you in a hurry?"

Harald was watching Norman, wondering how long it would be before the kid cracked. The lieutenant was trembling, skin seemed to be drawn tight over his cheek-bones, and a hot light burned in his eyes.

Norman sat down nervously by the chart panel. In his nervous state, the touch of something familiar gave him a feeling of solidity. The voices of the others irritated him.

"What do we do now?" he asked. "Just sit around and wait for it to happen?"

Merrill laughed bitterly. He and Harald exchanged amused glances. "Any better ideas, Mister?" Merrill asked ironically.

"Maybe I have," Norman snapped. "We might better do anything than just sit here."

Merrill got up and moved over to stare out the spaceport. His burns were paining him horribly; even the slight effort of limping across the control room was almost more than he could bear.

"Well, do something then. It's your baby. I'm resigning as of now ... in your favor."

"Do you mean that?"

Merrill nodded. Lines of repressed suffering marked his lean, wolfish face. "I don't think I'll be here long. Someone will have to take over. There's nobody else to rank you. Just a couple of radiation engineers and those armchair astronauts in our so-called crew. It's all yours, kid. But don't let it worry you too much."

Norman straightened and shook off his jumpiness. He looked around the control room and a ripple of sardonic amusement crossed his face. "My first command," he said. "A coffin ship full of corpses and doomed men. I'm sorry you're so—"

"It won't matter long," Merrill interrupted.

"Maybe it will. I think I have an idea. Can you maneuver this crate at all?"

"I guess we could. The forward propulsion jets are still all right. But the slightest acceleration might wreck things aft."

"What have we got to lose?" Harald asked. "What's on your mind, kid?"

If Norman was aware of the breach of discipline, he did not show it. His body leaned tensely over the chart panel as he pressed button after button, studying sheet after sheet. At last he raised his head. On his face was the expression of a small boy who has made an important discovery.

"Hidalgo," he said. "I was trying to remember what I knew about its orbit."

"Hidalgo? You mean that rogue asteroid which wanders as far out as Saturn's orbit?"

"Nobody ever goes there," Merrill put in. "There's some mystery about it—"

"We're going there ... if the ship holds together long enough. Just a minute and I'll figure your course. Sure you're in shape to handle the controls?"

Merrill limped to the instrument panel and began closing switches. "I hope you know what you're doing," he said roughly. Currents of vibration pulsed through the ship. With maddening slowness, the liner came out of her spinning drift and began to pick up speed. Norman ran through a list of figures and the third officer set the automatic controls.

A grotesque figure in radiation armor stood in the doorway.

"We're moving," it said through its amplifiers.

"This is Failles—radiation engineer—in charge of the men aft. We're trying to make Hidalgo."

"You'll never make it," Failles prophesied. "I came to report that the bulkheads are giving way."

Norman barked orders. "Merrill, keep an eye on the controls. Harald, you keep one on Merrill. And try to make contact with Scorpio. Tell them we're trying to make Hidalgo, to pass the word on to those freighters. Failles, I'll go with you and see what's up."

As Norman followed the nightmarish figure of Failles down the spiralling companion ladder, his mind worked feverishly to remember what he knew about Hidalgo. It was one of the minor planets, probably of the Trojan group originally, but its eccentric orbit and extreme inclination to the ecliptic stamped it as a rogue. At aphelion its distance from the sun was 9-1/2 units (nearly the orbit of Saturn) and its inclination 43-1/2 degrees. Three and a half years after perihelion it approached Jupiter's orbit closely.

Astronomical speculation was that its perturbations of orbit were caused by this near approach to Jupiter.

Norman came out of his reverie. Failles had stopped at a locker and gestured toward it. Radiation armor. Norman got the bulky garment from the locker and struggled into it.

They went down and down and down. A dizzy catwalk took them through the engine room where power was generated for the giant rocket ship, then down again, past passenger compartments into the waist hold, where the fantastic struggle against atomic degeneration was going on.

The microphone in Failles' helmet distorted his speech. "I don't think we can hold out much longer," he said. "The walls are so hot they're buckling and beginning to split."

"I don't understand all this," Norman said. "What's going on exactly?"

"Free radiation got into the fuel tanks," Failles explained. "You know that, of course. It started a chain reaction in the liquified fuel. The stuff degenerates slowly until it reaches a critical stage, then goes all at once. About a billionth of a second. Worse than that, it spreads through the rest of the metal parts. They begin to break down slowly, releasing energy in the form of heat or light, sometimes both. The light radiation kills, the heat corrupts the metal until it gives way, melting or crumbling depending upon its nature. Unless it hits a certain isotope first. In which case, blooey."

The scene was an inferno. Dark figures stumbled back and forth in the murk, armored men clumsily struggling with hoses and hand-pumping apparatus. The atomic-powered pumps had long since failed due to wild radiation. The threatened bulkhead was a mighty backdrop of pinkish coppery metal. An eery radiance played over the surface of the laminated plates. The men worked like maniacs deluging the walls and floor with liquified Rayburn's Isotope (a stabilizer) to damp out the degeneration, but already the plates were so hot that the stabilizer vaporized and was instantly dispersed through the room in sparkling clouds.

Even filtered by the Conklin glass of his helmet face-plate, the murky glare of the hold made Norman's eyes ache.

"How long do we have?" he asked.

The speaker in Failles' helmet rattled with a grunt. "That depends. The degeneration period varies according to the route it takes. There are three, possibly four routes in this case. I don't know which it will take. At the outside, five hours."

"We'll need at least three hours to reach Hidalgo," mused Norman.

"What good will it do to reach Hidalgo? We're taking an atomic bomb with us. If we land with this ship, it'll go with enough power to wipe Hidalgo out of existence and blow a hole in space to boot."

Norman frowned. "I thought of that. We won't try to land the ship. We'll have to abandon her and work our way down with the jet cartridges in our space suits."

Failles grimaced inside his helmet. "You can get awfully hungry in a space-suit, even if we can take enough spare tanks of air to hold out."

Norman nodded.

A figure detached itself from the huddled groups working the pumps and shuffled to the foot of the ladder. He pointed silently. Following his gesture, the pair looked at a corner of the bulkhead wall. A tear appeared, widened and ran down diagonally across the metal. Plates peeled off and fell like wax-paper crumbling in heat. Great blisters were rising on the surface of the wall. One broke and gouts of molten metal streamed down and spattered in a puddle. An uneasy suggestion of flow, of readjustment, of movement ran over the metal facing. More plates were grunting and buckling. They fell softly inward. More followed, dissolving rapidly as they came pelting down.

"Watch yourself!" Norman screamed. "She's going."

The place was an inferno. "She's going!" Norman yelled.

Liquid metal bubbled and spit. Runnels of magma pursued the retreating crewmen. A fiery surface lapped at the foot of the ladder.

Failles made an aimless gesture. "Get your men out of here," rasped Norman.

The huddle of dark figures broke and ran for the ladder. Air was blowing out of the hold in a shrill, whining scream. Norman was the last out. He slammed and clamped the door just as a rush of molten metal crashed against it.

"Keep fighting it," Norman ordered. "Compartment by compartment."

Walking was easier now that acceleration had begun to build into an approximation of normal gravity. Norman made his way back into the control room.

Crankily, the wreck of the Tellus swung through space. The forward drive jets were still functioning. Merrill shook his head as the framework and bulkheads creaked and groaned under the strain of acceleration.

"It'll be a miracle if she holds together an hour," he ground out.

"If it doesn't, we can stop worrying," Norman told him bluntly. "Have you an Interplanetary Astronaut for this sector?"

Merrill nodded toward the shelf where books were clamped.

Norman unsnapped Volume IV, and opened it to HIDALGO. Most of the information, especially astronomical data, he already knew; but a line at the bottom of the page caught his eye.

It is recommended that spaceships avoid this asteroid. Exploration has been impossible, for a number of reasons, and official charting expeditions have failed to return. No data available.

He read the notation aloud to the others.

"What do you suppose it means?" he asked.

"Could be that rough terrain and unstable rotation make a take-off impossible," Harald suggested.

Merrill's eyes narrowed. "I don't think so. Some of the other asteroids have been difficult enough that way. No, there's something different about Hidalgo. Maybe it's some kind of deadly radiations. I've thought a lot about it."

"You knew this all the time? Why didn't you say something about it?"

Merrill's habitual shrug was expressive. "It couldn't have mattered. Where else is there to go? I didn't think of it before you mentioned Hidalgo because I had no idea where it would be. In a way, I'm glad we're going there. You see ... my father commanded that charting expedition which was never heard from again. Now maybe I'll find out at last what really happened."

Norman lost all sense of time. The flight through space assumed the elastic dimension of nightmare.

He went aft again and checked with the radiation-fighters. There, the fight was going on in the engine room. It was at best a delaying action. Men dropped where they stood and were carried out. The lucky ones died of frightful burns where radioactive metal had spit through joints in their armor.

The speaker rattled inside his helmet as he addressed Failles. "If it spreads to the outside armor plates of the hull, we're done," he said.

Failles cackled. "It's already spread. They're glowing and beginning to buckle."

"Keep fighting it down."

"We can't. We're running short of Rayburn's Isotope."

"When it's gone, get your men into the dome-hold. There's an escape hatch there."

Harald looked up as Norman returned to the control room.

"I finally got Scorpio. These tubes are nearly burned out. I guess there's enough free radiation loose in this ship to fry eggs. The old man said they'd relay our message to the freighters. They'll check by Hidalgo to see if we made it."

Merrill was staring out the spaceport at the glittering darkness ahead.

"It's been nearly two hours," he said. "D'you think we'll be able to see it soon?"

"I doubt it. We're coming up on dark-side. Perhaps a faint radiance. Put everything on automatic, you two, and get into space suits. The others will meet us in the dome."

"Hull armor's going. We'll have to abandon ship. I hope we can raise Hidalgo. If not—"

Norman bent over the chart panel and checked his figures. He glanced at the indicator board. "I still get 11.18/4. And we're making incredible time. Maybe we'll make it—"

In the vast dome-hold at the nose of the hurtling liner were a group of burned and battered men. They grumbled hopelessly. Most of them were in bad shape.

Failles was at the spaceport. "No sign of Hidalgo," he reported.

"There won't be much to see," Norman warned him. "Try the magnascope."

Radiations were so powerful now that it was impossible to take the armor off the badly burned men long enough to tend their injuries. Thirty-one men still lived, but seven were seriously burned, at least one dying.

Time dragged hideously. In spite of the insulating layers, released energy from the degenerating metallic armor struck through the hold and built up heat alarmingly. Thermal indicators registered the temperature of a blast furnace. Automatic thermal adjustors inside the cumbersome armor could not react rapidly enough to keep up with the rising temperature.

Harald nudged Norman. He tried to look at his wrist-chron, but it had stopped from the heat.

"Better start negative acceleration," he said.

The lieutenant nodded. He and Harald fought their way back to the control room. Passageways were glowing, and metal rods felt pulpy even through their heavy gloves. The switches swung over to negative acceleration. The trip back to the dome was even more difficult.

The negative acceleration was taking its toll. Two of the injured men died.

Around the edges of each fused quartz spaceport was something like a rime of frost. It spread as they watched, spiderweb feelers reaching out across the circular panes. The faint starlight clouded and infinitely tiny points of radiance formed patterns within the crystalline surface.

"I'm going to open the airlock. Check your space suits."

One of the spaceports burst suddenly. Quartz-crystals showered into space. Air shrieked through the shattered port, freezing as it contacted the intense cold. Clouds of frost flecks formed and were instantly dispersed.

With the release of pressure, the airlock door came open easily. "There's a grey smudge down there," Merrill screamed, balancing precariously in the outer doorway. "Could that be Hidalgo?"

Norman was giving orders in a crisp, level tone. "Get the liquid-air tanks over-side. Failles, you take care of the casualties. Three of you should be enough. Harald, your job is to get the portable helioflash there safely. Merrill and the rest of you try to maneuver the air tanks down to Hidalgo. Use your jet cartridges sparingly, men, but—get there."

A shriek of terror came from Failles at the magnascope.

"The forward rocket tubes are fusing! They'll blow any time!"

"*Abandon ship!*"

In orderly fashion, the men lined up and went through the airlock. Norman went last.

Norman closed his eyes and shoved hard as he made the leap into space. The night seemed to open and swallow him. Impetus of his shove carried him away from the hurtling liner.

He opened his eyes as the giddiness of floating free in space swept over him. The nauseating agony of weightlessness wrenched at him. He retched painfully, but clenched his lips till the spasms died down. Fumbling, his fingers found the button which controlled the jet cartridges. With them, a spaceman has a limited maneuverability and control, even away from his ship. As he pressed the button, he prayed. They worked.

There was no sound, but a jarring vibration went through his body. It seemed an incredible distance to the air-tanks. Eight others were clustered around the bulky tanks when Norman reached them. Merrill was close behind him. Not far away was Harald, clutching the portable helioflash box to him.

Far below, slowly turning over as it came toward them, was the titanic wedge of barren rock which was Hidalgo. Then began a weary, heartbreaking task of jockeying the air-tanks into position and towing them to intercept the jagged wanderer of space.

Twenty men lived to reach it.

Failles and his helpers brought in all the injured, but only one was alive.

There was practically no gravity, so little that the centrifugal force of the spinning asteroid would have hurled the men back into space but for the magnetic soles of their armored shoes. Magnetic grapnels were attached to hold down the tanks. To make sure, lashings were run to up-thrust fingers of rock and everything loose made secure.

Clinging to a rope, Norman stood up and tried out the magnetic soles. They held, but it was necessary to shamble along without raising the feet any more than could be avoided. He looked about and his heart sank. No more eery and desolate place could be imagined. A ragged and uneven surface of bare rock and brittle obsidian-glass ended suddenly in a serrated horizon of ugly needle-point peaks. The horizon was disturbingly close. Overhead, the eternal stars moved in slow parade—but discernible motion—against the black vaults of space.

Just above the horizon was the sun, shrunken till its disk was barely perceptible as a disk. It shone feebly, but with harsh brilliance, casting solid shadows which moved like live things over the rough rocks.

Suddenly, Norman became conscious of something else. Another object moved swiftly out in space. A torpedo shape, faintly luminous.

Failles was pointing toward it. "The Tellus," he said grimly. "It's circling Hidalgo like a moon, coming down in a long spiral orbit. As its momentum decreases, it will come closer and crash. Looks as if we still have our wildcat by the tail."

Norman groaned. "When that stuff blows, it'll take this whole end of space with it."

Harald was crouching over his helioflash, working awkwardly at the dials with his heavy gloves.

"I'm trying to get Scorpio," he explained. "Tell them to warn off the freighters. No luck so far. These tubes are about shot. I can get a faint signal, but can't make out anything."

"Keep trying. We've got to warn off the freighters."

"I know. In spite of that faintness, the signal sounds as if it might be from fairly close."

Merrill came up. "I've been exploring," he said. "There's the wreck of a spaceship just over that ridge. Some sort of shaft close by it. I'm going over and look around."

He wandered off across the desolate stretch of rock. Norman watched him go, then turned to Harald. "You'd better follow and watch him. He's ready to crack. I'll take over the helio."

Failles shuffled up as Harald disappeared around a harsh shoulder of volcanic rock.

"Got through yet?" he snapped.

Norman shook his head. "I get a signal but they don't answer. It's too faint to make out."

"Let me try."

Norman gave way and Failles crouched down adjusting dials. He replaced a tube. The helio squawked savagely. The engineer fumbled over the knobs. The message clacked into his earphones.

"It's the freighter Dekorus," he shouted. "They're two days ahead of the others. Were on their way to Callisto when they got our distress helio from the Tellus. Couldn't reply. Their sender was out of order. They'll be here any time."

"For God's sake, stop that ship!" Norman screamed. "They'll get here just as that stuff blows...."

"I'm trying. They don't acknowledge my signals."

Like a racing moon, the wreck of the Tellus shot below the horizon. It seemed much closer than before.

"*Calling Dekorus. Why don't you answer, Dekorus? Calling Dekorus....*"

Two hours later, a solitary figure stumbled into the group around the helio. The instrument was silent. Men sat or crouched in stolid hopelessness. They had just pronounced sentence of death on themselves.

"We got through," Norman told Harald. "They aren't coming. Where's Merrill?"

Harald staggered and would have fallen, but Norman gripped him roughly.

"Merrill's dead," he said. A glaze of horror went over his face. "We found the ship. It was the one all right—his father's—the charting expedition. There was nothing in it—no bodies, nothing. We looked around. There was a hole there, a sort of shaft. It led down at a steep angle. A rough sort of ladder had been hacked into the rock, niches and pegs. We had a time getting down, but Merrill thought we might find something. He said he wanted to know before he died.

"We went down and down. And at the bottom was a door. It was a wooden door, of some wood I don't know, black and shiny with pinpoints of color here and there. And it was *carved*.

"While we stood there, it began to swing open. Slowly open. I was scared, frankly and honestly scared, but not Merrill. He strode up to it, shoved it open the rest of the way and went inside. I tried to follow, but my feet refused to move. I was rooted to the spot. I couldn't go in and I couldn't leave. It seemed hours. Then he came out. He came out running.

"I caught up with him and tried to hold him, but he struck at me and tried to kill me. When I looked in his eyes, I saw why. He was mad. Stark, raving mad. He broke away and ran to the foot of the stairs. But he didn't try to climb. He just kept banging his helmet face-plate on one of those rock pegs till it smashed. Have you ever seen a man smash his face plate in space? The horror of eyes squeezed out, flesh bursting to bloody pulp from the pressure of liquid blood inside, then in a second frozen steel-hard from the cold. It makes you all sick inside and you dream about it the rest of your life. But that wasn't the worst.

"I got curious about what he'd seen back there. I went back to have a look at it myself. The door was closed, but I pushed on it and it opened....

"One look was enough for me. I wish I could tell you what it was, but there aren't any words. Have you ever seen anything that made you want to die? I did. I took my look, then I got back here as fast as I could."

Norman stared into Harald's eyes, wondering if Merrill were the only one who had gone mad. Harald read the look and laughed bitterly.

"I wish I could go crazy," he said. "It might help. But I just want to die. After that, I couldn't go on living."

Norman glanced up as the Tellus, wreathed in eery radiance, shot above the horizon.

"It looks as if we'll all be dead soon enough to suit even you," he observed.

Harald came suddenly to life again. "The rest of you don't have to die," he shouted. "Contact that ship and tell them to wait for you. There's a self-propelled life boat intact in that wreck. It's not even dusty. Get going, man!..."

As the lifeboat roared out from Hidalgo, Norman was busy at the controls, maneuvering carefully to avoid the hurtling bulk of the derelict Tellus. He did not even realize what had happened till he heard the blast of air released from the airlock and someone raise a cry of "man overboard!"

It was Harald. From the ports, Norman could see him working the jets of his space-suit to intercept the racing bulk of the Tellus. Automatically his hands reached for the control bars, but Norman caught himself. He and Failles exchanged glances.

"It's a hard decision, lieutenant," Failles said. "But there isn't time. He said something about making sure, but I didn't know then what he meant."

"We know now," Norman gritted.

He shoved the switch-bars and gave the lifeboat full power. It roared into the darkness ahead.

Miles later, he and Failles stood by the stern ports and watched a fan of terrible lights spread across a quarter of the sky. Soundless, brilliant as the day-star, its glare struck through the ports like a solid force.

"Goodbye, Hidalgo," Norman mused aloud. "Goodbye, Harald. I wonder what he saw there that made him feel like that?"

"No one will ever know," Failles said.